Alyssa
the
Star-spotter
Fairy

To Isabella with lots of love

Special thanks to Rachel Elliot

ISBN 978-0-545-48481-7

Previously published as *Pop Star Fairies #6: Rochelle the Star Spotter Fairy* by Orchard U.K. in 2012.

All rights reserved. Published by Scholastic Inc., 557 Broadway, New York, NY 10012, by arrangement with Rainbow Magic Limited.

12 11 10 9 8 7 6 5 4 3 2 1   13 14 15 16 17 18/0

Printed in the U.S.A.   40

This edition first printing, March 2013

Alyssa
the
Star-spotter
Fairy

by Daisy Meadows

SCHOLASTIC INC.

It's about time for the world to see
The legend I was born to be.
The prince of pop, a dazzling star,
My fans will flock from near and far.

But superstar fame is hard to get
Unless I help myself, I bet.
I need a plan, a cunning trick
To make my stage act super-slick.

Seven magic clefs I'll steal —
They'll give me true superstar appeal.
I'll sing and dance, I'll dazzle and shine,
And superstar glory will be mine!

Contents

Showers and Sparkles!   1

Voice of an Angel   11

The Green Guy Trio   21

Tricks and Treats   33

Pesky Fairies!   43

Jack Frost Goes Goblin Hunting   55

Showers and Sparkles!

"Another gorgeous morning at the Rainspell Island Music Festival!" said Kirsty Tate happily. "Do you think I should wear this daisy headband today, Rachel?"

Her best friend, Rachel Walker, looked at their reflections in the big bathroom mirror.

"Definitely!" she said with a smile. "The white petals look so pretty against your dark hair."

The girls had just finished showering and getting dressed. They were camping at the festival with Rachel's parents, and they were all special guests of The Angels music group.

"I think you should wear my rose headband," Kirsty said, handing it to Rachel. "It will look great on you."

"I feel so lucky to be here," said Rachel as she arranged the headband in her

hair. "I've lost count of all the amazing things we've done — and the fabulous concerts we've been to!"

"Plus the fun we've had helping the fairies," said Kirsty with a twinkle in her eye.

No one knew that the girls were friends with the fairies of Fairyland. They had often helped the fairies outwit grumpy Jack Frost and his mischievous goblins. Soon after they had arrived on Rainspell Island, they met the Superstar Fairies, who used their magic clef necklaces to keep pop music sounding great. Jack Frost and his goblins had stolen the clefs and brought them to the festival to help Jack Frost become a superstar. So far, Kirsty and Rachel had helped five of the Superstar Fairies find their magic clefs.

"I just hope that we can find the final two missing necklaces before the end of the festival," said Rachel.

"Me, too," said Kirsty. "It would be terrible if Jack Frost ruined it for everyone. There are still lots of fantastic concerts to look forward to."

"Yes, I can't wait to see Jacob Bright at the Talent of Tomorrow show later," said Rachel. "He's one of the biggest up-and-coming stars here."

"And we still haven't seen Jax Tempo perform," said Kirsty. "I wonder when he'll be onstage. He must be very good to become so famous so quickly — I hadn't even heard of him until the festival started."

"Well, I'm ready," said Rachel. "Let's get our things and go back to the tent."

Kirsty put her hairbrush and spare headbands back into her bathroom caddy while Rachel went into the shower stall to get her shampoo.

5

But as she leaned over the shower drain, she noticed that the remaining bubbles were sparkling with rainbow colors. Rachel felt a tingle of excitement running up and down her spine.

"Kirsty!" she called. "Come over here. I think something magical is about to happen!"

Kirsty hurried eagerly into the stall, carrying her bathroom caddy and towel. The girls watched as the glistening foam grew fluffier and more colorful. Then there was a burst of suds, and a tiny fairy fluttered out of them.

6

"It's Alyssa the Star-spotter Fairy!" said Rachel with a big smile. "It's great to see you!"

"Hello, Rachel! Hello, Kirsty!" said Alyssa. "I'm so relieved that I found you! I've been searching everywhere for my magic clef necklace. Will you help me get it back from Jack Frost and his goblins?"

Alyssa gazed at them through her stylish glasses. Her eyes were full of hope, and her silver-gray dress shimmered in the lights of the shower stall.

"We'd love to," said Kirsty.

"Of course!" added Rachel.

"Thank you!" said Alyssa, clapping her hands together. "You see, my clef necklace helps people be confident in front of an audience. If I don't find it soon, all the stars at the festival will be too shy to perform."

"Oh, no!" said Kirsty. "If the stars can't perform, there won't be any more concerts. The festival will be ruined."

"Not only that," said Alyssa in a worried voice. "Without my clef, new superstar talent across the human world will never be discovered."

Before the girls could reply, they heard the door to the campground bathroom opening. Someone was coming in!

Voice of an Angel

Quickly, Alyssa darted into Kirsty's shower caddy. Just in time! A girl with dark, curly hair walked past the open door of the stall where the girls were standing. She was carrying a blue bag that read HOLLY on the side in white embroidered letters. She gave the girls a shy smile and went into a shower stall.

"Let's go," Rachel whispered. "We need to find somewhere private where we can talk to Alyssa."

Rachel picked up her shower caddy and towel, and she and Kirsty headed for the door. But just as they were about to leave, Kirsty heard something. "Wait," she said. "Listen!"

From the shower stall that Holly had walked into, there came a faint but beautiful sound. At first, the girls could hardly make out the words over the sound of the shower. But gradually the singing grew louder.

"That's an Angels song — 'Key to My Heart'!" Rachel exclaimed. "Do you remember the first time we heard it, Kirsty?"

"Of course I do," said Kirsty, smiling at her best friend. "It was at The Angels' charity concert, when we were helping Destiny the Rock Star Fairy."

Holly's voice grew even louder and more confident. "Wow!" said Rachel. "Holly's voice is amazing! She sounds like a real superstar."

They listened, entranced, until the song ended and the shower was turned off. Kirsty and Rachel burst into applause.

"You have an incredible voice!" said Kirsty, calling over the shower door. "I've never heard anyone sing like that before. You're wonderful!"

"Oh, thanks," said Holly, suddenly

sounding very shy. The girls heard her getting dressed. Then she came out, drying her long dark hair with a towel.

"Are you going to sing in the Talent of Tomorrow show later?" Rachel asked.

"I hope so — I
can't wait to
hear you sing
again!"

A delicate
blush rose in
Holly's cheeks.

"I don't think
so," she said.
"I love singing,
but not for an
audience. It's too
embarrassing."

"But you sang just now
while we were listening," Kirsty said.

"I thought you'd left," Holly said. "I
couldn't possibly perform on a stage
in front of hundreds of people. I'd be
too scared!"

15

Before the girls could try to persuade her any further, Holly hurried past them and left the showers. The girls stared at each other in surprise.

"I wish she realized how good she really is," said Rachel.

"Me, too," Kirsty replied. "But right now we have to help Alyssa. Come on!" They raced back to their tent and dropped off their shower supplies. Mr. and Mrs. Walker were making a pot of coffee on their little camping stove.

"Having a good time, girls?" asked Mr. Walker, smiling at them.

"Yes. Thanks, Dad," said Rachel, edging in front of her best friend.

Quickly, Kirsty opened her shower caddy. Alyssa zoomed up and hid under her hair.

"OK," Kirsty whispered to Rachel.

"See you later," called Rachel, waving at her parents.

"Are you leaving so soon?" said Mrs. Walker with a laugh. "Have fun!"

The best friends walked away from the tents and across the grass toward the outdoor concert stage. "It'll be quiet there," said Kirsty. "We can talk in private and make a plan to find Alyssa's missing clef."

But when they arrived at the stage, they found that it was already very busy. The Angels were there to prepare for the Talent of Tomorrow concert, and there were festival workers and technicians running around busily.

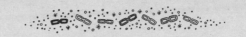

"We should tell The Angels about Holly," said Rachel. "Maybe they can persuade her to sing later."

"If Holly's going to have the confidence to sing for the audience, we need to get my magic clef back," Alyssa said from her hiding place. "Otherwise no one will be able to get her to her sing — not even The Angels."

As the girls neared the stage, they heard a soft voice singing in the wings.

"Sing it loud, sing it proud,
Sing for everyone to hear . . ."

"I know that voice!" Kirsty gasped. "It's Jacob Bright!"

The Green Guy Trio

The girls peeked into the wings. The handsome young singer was standing alone, practicing his new hit, "Sing It." But his voice was so soft that the girls could hardly hear him.

Just then, he noticed Rachel and Kirsty, and stopped singing at once.

"Hello," said Rachel excitedly. "You're one of our favorite superstars! We love your music!"

Jacob Bright blushed in embarrassment and turned away, mumbling something.

"That's weird," said Kirsty under her breath. "I'm surprised that such a big star is so shy."

Just then, they heard someone calling their names. They turned around to see The Angels waving at them.

"Hello!" said Emilia, coming over and

giving them a big hug. "How nice to see you here!"

"Are you getting ready for the Talent of Tomorrow concert?" Rachel asked. "We're really looking forward to it!"

The Angels looked at one another.

"I'm afraid we don't know if there's even going to *be* a concert," said Serena, her forehead creased with worry.

"What do you mean?" asked Kirsty. "Is it too hard to decide which singers to include?"

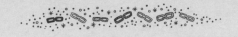

"Oh, I wish we had *that* problem," said Lexy. "This is far worse. Not one single person has signed up!"

"But there must be lots of people at the festival who want to be superstars," said Rachel in astonishment.

"That's what we thought," Serena said with a sigh. "Maybe we were wrong."

"No, you weren't wrong!" Kirsty exclaimed. "We met a girl today with a really beautiful voice . . . she was just too shy to sing in the concert."

"Listen, I bet you two are great at spotting talent," said Emilia. "Would you look around the festival for us and try to find some budding superstars?"

"We'd love to!" said Rachel.

"Thanks, girls," said Serena. "Come and find us later, and tell us who you've discovered!"

Rachel and Kirsty headed toward Star Village, the festival's cluster of activity tents.

"I'm so excited about talent-spotting for The Angels!" said Kirsty. "Alyssa, we're lucky to have you here — you'll be able to help us look for stars, and we can search for your magic clef at the same time!"

"I'd love to," said Alyssa. "Star-spotting is my favorite thing!"

As soon as the girls walked into Star Village, they saw a boy street dancing next to the makeup tent.

He was singing a cool hip-hop tune and practicing impressive shoulder pops and head spins. A few people had noticed him and were starting to gather around.

"He's got potential," whispered Alyssa.

But just then, the
boy noticed the
little crowd
around him.
He stopped and
stared down
at the ground,
shuffling
his feet.

"Don't stop!"
called out a girl
in the crowd.
"That was too cool!"

"Yes, we really liked it,"
said Rachel. "Please keep going — we're
looking for people to perform at the
Talent of Tomorrow concert, and you'd
be great!"

"No way!" said the boy, looking scared. "I couldn't do that." He walked away, and the three friends sighed. Everywhere they looked, they found the same problem. Near the Food Fest area, a girl was strumming her guitar beautifully. But as soon as they got closer, she put it down. People were singing, dancing, and playing instruments all over Star Village, but none of them wanted to perform in the talent concert.

"This is terrible," said Kirsty. "No one wants to perform at the concert — and there's no sign of Alyssa's magical clef, either."

"We'll have to go and tell The Angels," said Rachel. "I hate to disappoint them."

They walked slowly back to the stage. The Angels were still there, but this time they looked much happier. Jacob Bright was there, too, smiling broadly.

"Girls, we found an act for the talent show!" called Serena when she saw them. "They're absolutely fantastic — The Green Guy Trio!"

Up on the stage, three singers were confidently performing a

song. They were all dressed in bright green polo shirts, checked pants, and plaid caps made of wool with large bills that covered their faces. Each of them had a few moments in the spotlight, then gave a high five to the next member so that he could take his turn.

"At least there's one act for the Talent of Tomorrow concert," said Alyssa.

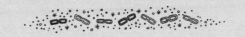

Rachel was staring at the band members' huge green shoes.

"How can they dance wearing those enormous shoes?" she wondered aloud.

"That's funny," said Kirsty. "I think they're passing something to one another when they do their high fives."

"Let me take a look," said Alyssa.

Keeping out of sight, she fluttered closer to the band. Then she came zooming back to the girls, her eyes wide.

"Rachel! Kirsty!" she gasped. "They have my magic clef!"

"Oh, my goodness!" said Rachel. "The Green Guy Trio is really three green *goblins*!"

Tricks and Treats

The goblins' song ended and, suddenly, there was a commotion backstage. The girls could hear someone shouting.

"I'll make you sorry you ever set eyes on that clef!" the voice snarled.

Then, the rising star Jax Tempo appeared onstage, his fists clenched in rage. He stomped toward the goblins,

who scrambled off the stage as fast as they could. Jax Tempo's ice-blue suit glittered in the sunshine.

"Get back here, you bunch of brainless blockheads!" he roared. "I'm

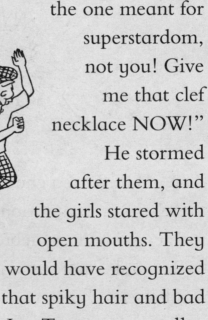

the one meant for superstardom, not you! Give me that clef necklace NOW!" He stormed after them, and the girls stared with open mouths. They would have recognized that spiky hair and bad temper anywhere. Jax Tempo was really Jack Frost in disguise!

"We have to get the magic clef from

the goblins before Jack Frost does," said
Alyssa in a panic. "Girls, it'll be easier if
you're both fairies, too."

Rachel and Kirsty nodded and looked
around. The Angels were deep in
conversation with Jacob Bright, and the
technicians were all busy checking
the spotlights.

"Let's go behind the stage
curtain," said Kirsty. "No
one will see us there."

The girls hurried onto
the stage and ducked
behind the blue curtain.
Then Alyssa flew out
from where she'd been
hiding under the daisy on
Kirsty's headband, already
waving her wand. Rainbow

sparkles burst from her wand's tip and
surrounded the girls in a glittering cloud
of color. Instantly, they shrank to fairy-
size and flapped their glittery wings,
twirling into the air in delight.

"Follow me!" called
Alyssa.

Together, the
girls and Alyssa
flew high above
the festival. It
was fun to look
down on the tents
and people below, all spread out like a
living, moving map.

"I hope no one looks up and sees us,"
said Kirsty.

"We're so high that we'll just look like
tiny dots to them," said Alyssa with a

smile. "We'll have to be careful when we fly down again, though."

"There's Jack Frost!" exclaimed Alyssa.

She pointed to the large crowd milling around Star Village. In the midst of all the people, they could see Jack Frost's ice-blue suit glittering. He was still stomping around, looking for the goblins and the magic clef.

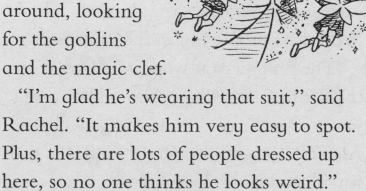

"I'm glad he's wearing that suit," said Rachel. "It makes him very easy to spot. Plus, there are lots of people dressed up here, so no one thinks he looks weird."

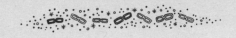

"If only the goblins were that easy to follow," said Kirsty. "How are we going to find them in this crowd? We don't even know which one of them has the clef."

"Wait a minute!" said Rachel. "Listen — can you hear someone singing?"

The three friends hovered in the air, listening. Above the cheerful buzz of the festival noise, they could hear a loud voice singing in perfect tune.

"That's Jacob Bright's song, 'Sing It'!" said Kirsty, remembering how they had heard him practicing in the stage wings.

"The only person who would have the confidence to sing that loud at the moment is the person with my clef," said Alyssa. "If we follow that sound, I'm sure it will lead us to the goblins!"

They zigzagged through the air, letting
the sound guide them. They ended up
in the Food Fest picnic area, and then
Rachel gave a shout.

"There they are!" she said, pointing to
three figures in green.

The goblins were taking turns singing
and dancing in the shade of a leafy tree.
They were still passing the magical clef
necklace back and forth as they gave one
another high fives.

Rachel, Kirsty, and Alyssa fluttered
lower. All the people in the area were
busy enjoying their
picnics, and no
one was looking
up. The fairies
hid themselves in
the leaves of the
tree above the goblins.

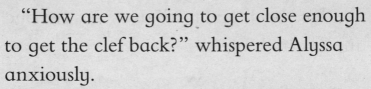

"How are we going to get close enough
to get the clef back?" whispered Alyssa
anxiously.

"These picnickers give me an idea,"
said Kirsty. "Alyssa, could you use your
magic to make a feast fit for a real
superstar? Goblins are always hungry.
I could be disguised as a server, and
try to get the clef back."

"Good plan, Kirsty!" said Rachel.

Alyssa waved her wand and a jet of
fairy dust swirled through the air. When
it hit the ground, a table sprang up. The
treats on the table looked and smelled
delicious. There were colorful cupcakes
on a three-tiered platter, a bowl of fizzy
green fruit punch, and an enormous
angel food cake topped with strawberries
and whipped cream.

"Now it's my turn," said Kirsty. "Wish
me luck!"

Pesky Fairies!

Kirsty fluttered down next to the table.
With another wave of Alyssa's wand,
Kirsty changed into a server from one
of the festival booths. She wore a
black dress and a little white apron.
Rachel and Alyssa flew down and hid
behind the large punch bowl. At that
moment, the wonderful smells of the food

reached the goblins' noses, and three
green faces peeked around the tree.

"Are you The Green Guy Trio?" asked
Kirsty in a cheerful voice. "We set up a
special feast for you, paid for by the
talent show organizers."

"Yes!" shouted
the goblins,
scrambling over
one another
toward the
tempting food.

As they
greedily shoved
cupcakes into
their mouths, Kirsty
took a step closer.

"Um, I was wondering . . . would you
sing for me?" she asked. "Everyone says

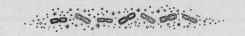

that you have amazing voices, but I
haven't heard you yet."

Hidden behind the punch bowl, Alyssa
and Rachel were listening to every word.

"That's a smart idea," whispered
Alyssa. "Whichever goblin
is willing to sing for
her must have my
magic clef!"

Eager to show off,
one goblin started
singing. He sounded
like a true superstar!

"He's the one!" said
Alyssa.

She and Rachel zoomed out of their
hiding place toward the goblin. They
could see the magic clef clutched in his
hand! But just as Rachel was reaching

out to touch it, one of the other goblins cried out in alarm.

"Fairies!" he yelled. "Horrible, tricky, pesky fairies!"

Quickly, the singing goblin threw the clef to him, and they both disappeared into the festival crowd. The third goblin was too busy munching on the angel food cake to bother running off. Kirsty ran after the two goblins with the clef, leaving the third one to enjoy the feast. Rachel and Alyssa zoomed overhead, trying to keep the goblins in sight.

"They're heading for Star Village," said Rachel. "I've got an idea!"

She and Alyssa swooped down and tucked themselves under Kirsty's hair.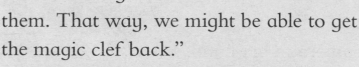

"Listen," Rachel said quickly. "The goblins love being flattered. Let's dress up as fans of The Green Guy Trio — then they're sure to let us get close to them. That way, we might be able to get the magic clef back."

"I think that could work," said Alyssa. "But we'll have to get out of sight for me to do my magic."

Kirsty darted behind a deserted tent, and Rachel and Alyssa flew out. The little fairy waved her wand at her human friends and chanted a spell.

"Help me foil the goblins' plans.
Make these girls true Green Guy fans!"

A stream of fairy dust instantly transformed Rachel and Kirsty! Rachel grew back to her normal size, and both girls found themselves wearing green dresses and green wool hats, like the goblins'. Kirsty had a little video camera in her hand.

"We look just like fans!" said Rachel

with a giggle. "Now we just have to find
the goblins."

Alyssa hid in Rachel's pocket, and
then the girls ran through Star Village.
Almost immediately, they spotted a flash
of green in the crowd. The two goblins
were hurrying along.

"Keep a lookout for
fairies!" they heard
the taller one say.

"It's The Green
Guy Trio!"
squealed Kirsty
at the top of
her voice.

"Stop!" shrieked
Rachel. "We're
your biggest fans!"

They raced after the goblins, who stopped and grinned at them in delight.

"Can we videotape you?" asked Kirsty, holding up the camera. "This is very exciting!"

"Sure," said the taller goblin with a little swagger. "Anything for our fans." Rachel stood beside the two posing goblins as Kirsty filmed them.

"It would be so cool to get you singing on tape," said Rachel. "Please, would you sing for the camera?"

Eagerly, the shorter goblin took a step forward and launched into "Sing It." He must have the magic clef! Alyssa flitted out from Rachel's pocket to get it, but the tip of her wing brushed against the goblin's arm. On the alert for fairies, the goblin yelped and darted into the crowd, without even waiting to tell his singing partner why he had run away. "Hey!" the taller goblin shouted after him.

"Never mind him!" said Kirsty quickly. "Everyone knows that you're the real star of the band!"

The goblin smiled smugly. Because of the video camera, a small crowd had started to gather, thinking that the goblin must be really famous. The girls were able to slip away without him noticing.

"We have to catch up with that goblin," said Rachel. "If Jack Frost finds him first, we could lose the clef forever!"

As soon as they were out of sight, Alyssa turned Kirsty and Rachel back into fairies again. They zoomed up into the air and looked around.

"I see him!" cried Kirsty. "He's heading toward the campsite!"

They chased the goblin toward the field full of little tents. Luckily, it wasn't very busy because most people were exploring the festival. The goblin rushed between the tents, and the girls darted after him. Somewhere nearby, they could hear someone singing. It sounded like Holly!

The goblin was a very fast runner, and the girls were getting tired. Just then, Rachel gave a cry of alarm and pointed into the distance. Someone was striding toward the campsite — someone in an ice-blue suit. He had spiky hair, and he was clenching his fists.

"It's Jack Frost!" exclaimed Kirsty. "And he's looking for the goblin!"

Jack Frost Goes Goblin Hunting

The goblin spotted Jack Frost at
exactly the same moment. He froze
in his tracks and started to shake. The
girls caught up with him, and he looked
at them with big, scared eyes.

"Don't let him find me!" he squeaked.
"He's going to be so angry, and I hate it
when he shouts!"

Even though the goblin had caused lots of trouble, the girls felt sorry for him.

"Our tent is close by," said Rachel. "You can hide in there if you like."

"Yes!" said the goblin. "Quick, hide me, please!" He was too scared of Jack Frost to worry about the fairies now.

Rachel and Kirsty flew ahead and led him to their tent.

"I hope Mom and Dad are out," said Rachel under her breath.

Luckily, the tent was empty. The goblin scurried inside, and the three friends swooped after him and zipped

the tent flap closed. The goblin sat down in the middle of the tent. Outside, they could hear Jack Frost getting closer.

"I know that goblin came this way," they heard him mutter. "I saw his footprints. I'm going to search every single tent until I find him, and then I'll make him sorry he stole from me!"

When he heard this, the goblin started shaking again. Bravely, Rachel flew over to him and perched on his knee.

"Listen to me, goblin," she said. "We can help you escape. Alyssa can use her magic to send you to the other side of the festival grounds. But if you want our help, you have to help us, too. Give back the magic clef necklace. It doesn't belong to you."

The goblin thought about it for a moment.

"If I give you the necklace, you'll help me escape?" he asked.

The three fairies nodded. Outside, Jack Frost's stomping footsteps were getting louder.

"All right!" cried the goblin. "I'll do it."

He thrust the clef toward Alyssa, and it immediately shrank to fairy-size.

"You did the right thing," Kirsty promised the goblin.

"I don't care about that," he snapped. "Just get me out of here!"

Alyssa waved her wand. In a rainbow-colored flash, the goblin disappeared to the other side of the festival — just as the tent flap whipped open. Jack Frost's furious face appeared in the entrance.

"You're too late," said Rachel,

putting her hands on her hips. "Alyssa
has her clef back."
"You horrible,
interfering
fairies!" Jack
Frost yelled.
"You'll be
sorry you ever
crossed me! I
still have the
last clef, and
that means I can
ruin your precious
concert tomorrow —
and all the concerts everywhere!"
Giving them a final scowl, he
disappeared in a bolt of icy lightning.
"Thank goodness he's gone," said
Kirsty with a sigh.

"You've both been amazing," said Alyssa, hugging them tightly. "Thank you for getting my clef back. Now you'll be able to enjoy the Talent of Tomorrow concert — my clef will give the singers the courage to perform!"

She returned Kirsty and Rachel to their normal size and fastened the clef around her neck.

"I'm going back to Fairyland to tell the other Superstar Fairies the good news," she said.

"Good-bye, Alyssa!" said the girls. "It was fun spotting new stars with you!"

At the Talent of Tomorrow show that evening, the mood was electric. All the talented performers that the girls had spotted earlier had signed up for the show. Rachel and Kirsty were in the front row with Rachel's parents. They cheered and clapped for the hip-hop artist and the guitar player. The audience was on their feet, whistling and whooping. Then The Angels walked onstage to introduce the next act.

"Now we're delighted to present a duo that will rock your world," said Emilia.

"That's right," Lexy added. "These guys sound awesome on their own, but together, they're dynamite."

"And you're lucky enough to be here for their first duet," said Serena. "Give it up for Jacob Bright . . . and Holly Day!"

Spotlights swept across the stage and fireworks exploded in time to the music. Jacob and Holly walked out side by side, and launched into Jacob's latest hit.

Everyone listened as Holly's voice soared out, clear and confident.

"What an amazing voice!" exclaimed Mrs. Walker. "She's definitely a star in the making."

"I think Mom wants to be a star-spotter, too," said Rachel with a giggle. She and Kirsty raised their arms in the air and swayed as they sang along to the chorus:

"Sing it loud, sing it proud,
Sing for everyone to hear . . ."

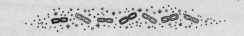

Just then, something made Rachel turn around. A few rows behind them, she saw the three goblins in their Green Guy Trio outfits, arms raised and swaying. She nudged Kirsty, who looked back and smiled.

"They seem to be enjoying themselves too much to cause any trouble right now," she said.

The event was a huge success. But Rachel and Kirsty knew that Cassie the Concert Fairy's magic clef was still missing. It was up to them to get it back from Jack Frost and his goblins — or the festival finale would be ruined!

Alyssa has her magic clef back.
Now Kirsty and Rachel need to help

Cassie
the Concert Fairy!

Read on for a special sneak peek. . . .

Trouble on Rainspell Island

"My autograph book is almost full," said Kirsty Tate, turning the blue pages happily. "We've met so many famous stars at the festival!"

"Mine, too," said Rachel Walker, who had her pink autograph book open on her lap. "I can't believe it's our last day already."

"The Rainspell Island Music Festival has been so much fun, I can hardly imagine going back to ordinary life," said Kirsty with a laugh. "I wish it didn't have to end."

Kirsty and Rachel were sitting on stools outside their tent. They had really enjoyed being special guests of their favorite music group, The Angels. The afternoon sun seemed to light up the tents around them with a golden glow.

"It looks like it's enchanted, doesn't it?" said Rachel. "Almost as magical as the fairy campsite we visited with Jessie the Lyrics Fairy."

Kirsty and Rachel were good friends with many fairies, and they had often visited Fairyland and ruined Jack Frost's evil schemes. On the first day of the festival, they had stumbled across one of his most mischievous plans yet. Jack Frost had stolen seven magic music clef necklaces from the Superstar Fairies. He planned to use them to become a superstar himself.

He had given most of the clefs to his goblins, who brought them to the Rainspell Island Music Festival. There, Kirsty and Rachel had tracked them down one by one. Jack Frost had disguised himself as rapper Jax Tempo to impress people at the festival, but he didn't fool the girls for long.

The Superstar Fairies needed their clefs to look after superstars everywhere, and Kirsty and Rachel were determined to help their friends. So far, they had helped six fairies get their magic clefs back, but Jack Frost still had one. It belonged to Cassie the Concert Fairy. . . .

RAINBOW magic ™

Three Books in Each One— More Rainbow Magic Fun!

Joy the Summer Vacation Fairy
Holly the Christmas Fairy
Kylie the Carnival Fairy
Stella the Star Fairy
Shannon the Ocean Fairy
Trixie the Halloween Fairy
Gabriella the Snow Kingdom Fairy
Juliet the Valentine Fairy
Mia the Bridesmaid Fairy
Flora the Dress-Up Fairy
Paige the Christmas Play Fairy
Emma the Easter Fairy
Cara the Camp Fairy
Destiny the Rock Star Fairy
Belle the Birthday Fairy
Olympia the Games Fairy
Selena the Sleepover Fairy
Cheryl the Christmas Tree Fairy
Florence the Friendship Fairy
Lindsay the Luck Fairy

■ **SCHOLASTIC**

scholastic.com
rainbowmagiconline.com

HIT entertainment

RMSPECIAL10

RAINBOW magic

These activities are magical!
Play dress-up, send friendship notes, and much more!

SCHOLASTIC
www.scholastic.com
www.rainbowmagiconline.com

HIT entertainment

RMACTIV3

RAINBOW magic™

There's Magic in Every Series!

The Rainbow Fairies
The Weather Fairies
The Jewel Fairies
The Pet Fairies
The Fun Day Fairies
The Petal Fairies
The Dance Fairies
The Music Fairies
The Sports Fairies
The Party Fairies
The Ocean Fairies
The Night Fairies
The Magical Animal Fairies
The Princess Fairies
The Superstar Fairies

Read them all!

■ SCHOLASTIC

scholastic.com
rainbowmagiconline.com

HiT entertainment

RMFAIRY